The Princess of Central Park

First published in the United States of America

By Createspace.com, 2013

Copyright George Sorbane 2013

Library of Congress Control Number

2013914627

DISCLAIMER

Some of the language contained in the book "The Princess of Central Park" may be offensive to some readers. The opinions of the characters in this book do not necessarily reflect the opinions of the author or the publisher. The book has to be read in its entirety to discern the underlying messages in it. Any resemblance of the characters, past or present, to actual individuals is completely coincidental with the exception of well-known historical figures.

The Princess of Central Park

Table of Contents

Search of a Lifetime

May 3, 2007.

A tall young man sporting a khaki military jacket entered Columbia University's Chapel of St. Paul, kneeled down, made the sign of the cross and then sat down calmly, concentrating his thoughts and feelings on a day that had so much meaning to him.

Thirty five years ago, his father, Air Force Major Douglas Meecham Stafford II was shot down by a Russian SAM Missile over Haiphong Harbor, Vietnam on a mission to suppress enemy fire that had been badgering air attacks by US forces.

Doug's mother Isabel, the only child of a prominent Napa Valley winery owners, had suddenly fallen into a world of cryptic sadness and depression, unable to understand why cruel fate had taken away her man, a man she loved more than anything in the world.

Just twenty-two years old, with a year old baby in her hands and unable to suppress the pain of losing him, she found solace in her hippie friends, now part of a raging anti-war movement. Isabel did not realize that entering the imaginary world of drugs was a deadly illusion, whereby one can separate from reality by ascending into a heavenly dream, just to descend into a spiral of suffering without an end in sight.

Her journey came fast and brutal, as she succumbed to drugs and died of overdose in the hippie colonies of Northern California. Young Doug was left in the care of his Aunt Hattie Meecham Stafford, a professor of English Literature at Columbia, an accomplished socialite and political power broker who had personally met all United States Presidents since General Dwight Eisenhower.

Spending his youth in some of the most prestigious private schools and having wealth and social standing that would have made anybody in the world turn green with envy did not make the young man any happier. On the contrary, it gave him a view of a life immersed in loneliness, even though he was one of world's most eligible bachelors with an estimated net worth of five billion dollars.

Mother Hattie, as Doug called her, raised him in a home full of unconditional love and devotion, trying not to cry when he failed and celebrated every little victory he would accomplish. She always encouraged him to be bold and independent but compassionate and kind, a task that his godfather Robert Weisberg was happy to share.

After graduating from Yale with a degree in business, Doug started his professional life as a floor trader in the Meecham Holdings flagship 5th Fund, which included large properties on both coasts and portfolio of stocks in the billions. At the age of 26, he fell in love with mezzo-soprano

Heather Wertheim, one of the world's most beautiful and gifted women, yet the relationship soon petered out into a polite but hollow friendship, his heart unable to share life with someone that was distant and cold, failing to sense the enormous peaks and crevices of his soul.

"I don't want to spend my life surrounded by yes men and boot lickers cuddling me because of my wealth, sleep in a house bigger than my high school and marry a cold hearted gold digger with a perfect Miss USA smile," Doug would say angrily.

"I simply need a hug from time to time, a hug of love, just for me and only me."

Millions of people on this planet would have given everything to have his prestige and power, and all Doug was dreaming of was to be able to visit Mom and Dad on Saturday, get a hug or two and perhaps take them out for a nocturnal dinner, just to feel the warmth of being with his loving family.

His immersion in the endless enigmatic study of the human experience finally turned into a spiritual experiment, a search of why some of us turn out to be servants of a merciful God and others tools of a merciless Evil. Doug's trek led him to the Columbia Doctorate of Sociology Program and Professor Samuel Goldring, a man Mother Hattie did not care much about. After nearly four years of extensive course studies and having passed all the required exams, it was time to sit down with his academic adviser and discuss possible research topics in his domain of interest, the study of the enigma of the human mind.

After hearing Doug's story, Dr. Goldring offered some philosophical "modus operandi" in search for a driver of motives and lives of people at large, and how they can be used to shape the research needed to complete his dissertation.

"You need to take statistical samples from socio-economic groups that encompass your field of research interests, for example, ever growing groups of homeless Americans that have fallen on hard times. Look for non-parametric trends and descriptions that affirm the hypothesis you have postulated to start with, then create a statistical model describing all events under observation with a high degree of correlation. "

"Consider the sub-groups of people living in Central Park at this instance. Sampled for past income level, age group, health level, gender and criminal history, what was the reason they found themselves in this predicament, and for how long? "

"You will have to change a social status, live with them, gain their trust and then determine the values of those attributes in order to accept or reject a hypothesis regarding prevailing social trends at that time."

Walking down the alley, Doug was already wondering how to break the news to Mother Hattie regarding his new adventure.

"I have to be slow and careful in my

approach so she does not get upset or start crying, knowing that I will be sleeping under open sky with people who have nothing to lose," he thought, putting on the happiest face one can imagine.

But she had other plans.

"Douglas, would you please take me to the Met for this Friday's presentation of Tosca, would you please darling? It has been an eternity since I have seen a decent opera troupe."

"Certainly, Mother Hattie, of course," Doug gladly agreed.

"I will get to it immediately and reserve your favorite VIP booth. Would you mind if we invite Heather to come with us so she won't be sad and feel abandoned again, would you Mother?"

"I love to share that marvelous evening with her, darling, if she can take a break from her busy schedule. You know that I adore everyone that loves my boy."

Doug waited till Friday night to disclose his secret caper, to Mother Hattie's great chagrin and displeasure. During the intermission, as if the Providence wanted to give her a shoulder to cry on, they stumbled onto Mayor and Mrs. Weisberg, accompanied by police commissioner Mitch Murphy and a few associates from the security detail.

"Robert and Carla, how happy to see you again, sweethearts! And you also, Mitch! Enjoying the Opera? They are wonderful and gifted, aren't they?" Mother Hattie exclaimed joyfully, hiding behind a smile her deep unease with Doug's planned journey into madness.

"By the way Robert, and with sincere apologies for marring such a charming evening, I must let you know that Doug has contemplated an absolutely atrocious plan to spend some six months in Central Park, masquerading as a partially blind homeless person, in order to collect observations required by his academic adviser Dr. Goldring. I hate this man and I am quite sure that he invented this monstrosity."

"He had nothing to do with it, Mother Hattie, it was my idea to infiltrate the homeless community to finish my graduate work," Doug countered tensely.

Clouds of doubt and suspicion appeared in Mayor Weisberg's eyes.

"You, Douglas Meecham Stafford III, the only heir of a NY dynasty with an estimated net worth of five billion dollars, a man whose mother's family owns 1/4 of State of California wine country and had incalculable contributions to this city's civil and cultural institutions, you will spend six months as a homeless person in a park full of boozers, druggies and dirt bags? I have not told you this thing before, Hattie, but NYPD is looking for a crazy woman that had threatened people with a silver envelope opener, isn't that right Murphy? And the other day, someone was attacked with a staple gun, so it took twenty six stitches to separate his behind from his trousers."

"I already warned Doug about the dangers he may face, but he would not listen to me," Mother Hattie charged.

"I don't know if I can survive for six long hot months, looking at the park through my living room windows and wondering if Doug could be attacked at any moment by some lunatic or criminal," she almost cried in despair.

"What do you think, Commissioner Murphy? What can we do to make sure this man can be secure, if not always, at least most of the time? Vividly remembering his father and grandfather, may they rest in peace in the Republican part of Heaven, I know for sure he won't back down, no matter what," Mayor Weisberg finally conceded.

Commissioner Murphy had a plan for action.

"First, Doug has to come to my office so that I can make him an honorary captain of NYPD and introduce him to Lt. La Paglia, chief of plainclothes security around Central Park with his twenty officers always on duty. Then we have to issue a miniature radio with a panic button and transponder in case of abduction. Lastly, a set of Kevlar pants and jacket may come handy just in case the staple gun attacker strikes again."

"Hattie, would you please remind this young man to show up in Commissioner Murphy's office at 9 AM sharp this coming Monday? I will see you later Doug, that's a promise. Okay?"

"And before you go, Robert, listen to this," Mother Hattie added warily.

"Doug had conspired with Dr. Bagelman, our eye doctor, to have a set of special slightly scratched brown eye lenses prescribed so he would appear partially blind, just to make his cover believable. Isn't that insanity? Please tell him to stop being a trouble maker and think about me, lonely me," Mother Hattie pleaded breathlessly, as Mrs. Weisberg offered her a hug of compassion.

Mayor Weisberg covered his eyes in a sign of complete disbelief and reticent confusion.

"Hattie dear, I cannot take this any longer, but my office will be in touch with the police at all times, just to make sure they have this young man in plain view and free from harassment and danger of any kind. That's something I can promise with certainty, okay dear?"

"Take care of yourself, young man, and stay away from envelope openers and staple guns, would you, please?" Mayor Weisberg advised before leaving.

Come Monday morning, Doug was in Commissioner's Murphy's office, meeting with Lt. La Paglia and briefed by other officers from Central Park security detail.

He was fitted with all the gear assigned to him, feeling like a police robot ready to strike yet having trouble coping with the heat.

"This better turn all right," he thought

angrily, feeling uncomfortable with the Kevlar pants and jacket.

"I already feel like I'm in a coffin, hot and tense for no reason at all."

Doug had no idea how dangerous and unpredictable the end of his journey will turn out to be, a journey of penetration into social circles, which many friends and advisers had warned him not to even consider. Still, being a stubborn Irishman, he dismissed all threats and charged ahead into the unknown.

The Princess of Central Park

First Day on the Job

At 5:15 AM on a crisp March morning, 2009, Doug carefully opened the side door of the Meecham building on West 82nd street and Central Park West, looked suspiciously around to make sure no one is watching, then pushed out a shopping cart with all his earthly possessions and started slowly walking away until he could see the windows of Mother Hattie's apartment. He had left a tripod and a set of Barska long-range binoculars in her living room, so she could observe his journey from a distance whenever she felt lonely or worried by people wandering on both sides of the street.

There were already some folks jogging around and the usual taxicabs hustling to pick a fare but not many homeless people in sight, so he decided to find a lonely tree trunk to lean on and take a quick nap before the morning madness of New York took a hold.

An unshaved man in his early thirties with scattered brown hair, peculiar bow tie and a look of a college professor approached silently.

"I am Stan Woramcke," he said softly after covering himself with a white and gray Azteca blanket.

"Doug here, very nice to meet you, Professor."

"I actually taught for a while in Yale and Columbia, hoping to get a job as an assistant curator in some of the museums around New York area until the break up with my girlfriend last year," Woramcke explained, his big eyes full of tears.

Born and raised in an educated family in Chicago, Stan had been diagnosed with intestinal flatulence in his teens, an extremely rare disease that unless treated promptly, could produce bursts of gas leading to very real life complications. A lifelong Republican, he had struck a relationship with a pollster of the Clinton campaign, an older woman that was kind and willing to help him cope with life's never ending challenges, including his embarrassing health issues and ever present habit to save a penny for a rainy day.

Stan had been rejected for a position of assistant curator at the Metropolitan Museum of Art, the job instead going to a Chinese born Master of Arts candidate named Fu Fong, after being told by the politically correct chair of the selection committee Dr. Lasker, "Mr. Fong is more likely to be representative of the people visiting our Museum."

Woramcke was heart broken and offended by the snub.

After finding a part time position in Brooklyn's school district, he embarked on a mission of revenge against Mr. Fong and his guardian angel Dr. Lasker. For centuries, Woramcke's family had lived on the border between Poland and Germany, so deeply buried in his genetic code, there was a memory gene of a recipe for making turnip, red beets and lentil soup, a mixture creating enough gas to propel a small homemade rocket.

So he would study carefully his foes' museum schedules, then show up and wait until the curator discussed with a group of almost religious admirers a famous art work by Renoir or someone alike, giving Woramcke the extreme pleasure of releasing a skunkish fart and then melt in the crowd, leaving his enemies sinking in embarrassment and despair.

Stan did not realize that his psychopathic anger had earned him the dubious distinction of being the first living chemical weapon on US soil, anger that subsided when the deepening relationship with the pollster woman took a front seat in his life.

But the ideological war that was unleashed in the election following the 2008 market crash took a toll on their affair that was ominous and hurting. One day before the Presidential election, a major scuffle broke out between the two. Dr. Woramcke, who had a well-documented habit of annoying people, went over the line after hearing his love predicting that Obama would be the winner.

He had prepared a stack of pancakes for her and two over easy eggs plus half a can of Sheba cat food sautéed in mushrooms and vegetables for himself, the other half of the can given to his cat Mina. The woman was outraged by his blatant stinginess.

"Idiot, religious cash register," she screamed at him.

"Can you Republicans once in a lifetime stop thinking about money, get yourself a decent breakfast and accept a defeat?"

So she threw all his possessions in hallway, changed the locks and Dr. Woramcke had suddenly become a street person, no medicine or money at all, at the mercy of complete strangers.

Doug carefully peeled off the sticker from Stan's medicine bottle.

"I will have my aunt take a look at your prescription and see if she has some of those. Her medicine cabinet is full with stuff," he said as Woramcke retreated to his part of the park.

Doug must have snoozed for the best part of an hour and a half in a crisp silence, punctuated by screeching brakes, honking of cars and people screaming in foreign languages, when he felt someone gently rubbing a piece of cold metal right under his chin.

Opening his eyes, he saw the speckled face and dirty, clustered hair of a woman in her early 30s, blackened front tooth, whispering in a raspy, broken voice, "You are leaning on my tree, you young punk, the tree of Lucy Brave, holding a envelope opener right under your beautiful face and just about to slash your throat from ear to ear."

"Oh my, I see a pair of brown eyes, perhaps I should gouge your stupid eyes out, you white piece of trash, don't you know that I hate brown eyed men, don't you?"

Doug tried to mutter an apology, but the suddenness and hostility of the encounter had left his throat dry and lips numb, thoughts scattered like a flock of birds downed by a hungry eagle.

"Princess Lucy, my darling Princess Lucy, I have few treats for you, blueberry muffins, your favorite," a voice with a pronounced foreign accent sang the words gently. The blade left Doug's chin and she turned around.

"Oh, is that you Lutvi, trying to bribe me from doing justice to this invader, are you?"

"Of course, Lucy darling, of course, you know I love you and always will, that's why I bring flowers, donuts and other nice things. Would you please forgive this young man, today, just today, he being new and not knowing the rules of your palace?"

Lucy turned to Doug, opener in hand.

"Do you see those four trees out there? This is my palace, and no one but no one is allowed in. Are you listening to me? You have a name, brown eyes?"

"Doug, Madam, Doug," he whispered respectfully.

When Lucy retreated to her private chambers with the blueberry muffins, he noticed with the corner of his eyes a middle aged man, right hand under the jacket, some thirty feet behind Lutvi.

"My God, this must be one of Lt. La Paglia's men, ready to take this woman down," he thought in a flash of panic.

Unsuspecting Lutvi, kind and smiling, sat on a bench nearby, ready for a talk with this newcomer in the world of Central Park homeless inhabitants.

He had quite a story to tell, as Doug soon found out.

Lutvi Bezirganov turned out to be a former thief from a small Central Asian Republic, jailed for stealing horses when the revolt against long time Soviet puppet Ismail Dudaev exploded, sending hordes of angry citizens on an assault of a police station where he was being held.

Very shrewd Lutvi arranged to have a picture of himself snapped by the foreign press as a bunch of revolutionaries of the "New Islamic World" stormed the presidential palace, just to find themselves helpless against the Russian troops that have rolled into the capital city. When the forces of Ismail Dudaev returned to power, Lutvi ran to the American embassy and requested help and protection. Eager to help usher a "New Arab Spring" of dynamic evolution in the Islamic world, the Americans were delighted to grant a political asylum based on a wealth of evidence supporting his claim of leading an uprising against the Soviet puppets, hence sending Lutvi to Turkmenistan and then right to New York.

The first impression of American life was decidedly negative to Lutvi: he could see only two horse carriages around Central Park, plenty of homeless people around and scores of folks dressed in the strangest clothes he had ever seen, many enjoying generous servings of ice cream or munching on other goodies.

Religious and racial anger erupted in his lonely heart.

"Overfed American dogs, children of Sheitan," he thought in disdain.

"You don't even have horses to ride in such a beautiful city, instead using bunch of taxicabs ran by obnoxious Pakistani and Jamaican bandits."

Yet the coldest streets of New York were warmer than the summer jail of Dudaev, so Lutvi accepted enthusiastically his new destiny when it became clear that the horse shortage around town was dwarfed by a multitude of depressed and lost Russian women completely unable to fit in this tightly regulated chaos called America, an observation that grew a devilish business plan in his practical mind.

He met a friend of his, Sasha Murkin, a Russian thief who had stolen a fuel truck from a Spetsnaz camp in Chechnya, just to be caught by the soldiers and get the beating of his life. After spending three months wrapped up in sheepskins coated with balsamic oils under the care of a local shaman, he managed to slip into the neighboring republic during the revolt against Ismail Dudaev, joining his friend Bezirganov in the attack on the presidential palace.

After the brutal crackdown on the Resistance by Dudaev's troops, he applied for and was granted an asylum in the US as a young revolutionary who had risked his life fighting with the cronies of the Soviet supported establishment.

Murkin, a graduate of Moscow State University with a degree in Statistics, was never able to use his scientific skills due to an insatiable urge to borrow things from other people without any intention of returning them, a fatal weakness that had almost cost him his life.

Lutvi's observation regarding the multitude of lost and depressed Russian women had grown into a brilliant plan in his enterprising brain: he would provide a network of call girls and Sasha was to create a system of drivers and safe houses where the rendezvous would take place.

To keep a low profile, Bezirganov, Murkin & Co had rented a storefront down on 75th street and opened a Russian pastry store ran by Sasha's former wife Lyudmila, an ideal front to run a business without attracting the attention of the police.

Many of ring's customers were from former Soviet Block diplomatic missions while others were simply low-level Communist apparatchiks or plain street toughs, prone to violence and lawless behavior. Frequent fights and threats against the girls forced Lutvi to hire master of jiu jitsu and former Mongol police captain Babul Unkur as a bodyguard, driving his bosses around town in a low mileage red Toyota truck, proudly sporting a smashed driver's side door and a green tailgate.

So Lutvi and Sasha would rotate in and around Central Park, closely monitoring arrivals and departures of the girls to and from customer rendezvous, then would stop by the store to make sure money was deposited as required. All women were expected to purchase some pastries with proceeds from a visit and then get reimbursed for it, a carefully designed tactic by Murkin to avoid an arrest by the Vice Squad in case of a leak or betrayal by some of the girls and create an illusion that this was a good fate business establishment, just in case of an audit by the cops.

"So far I have done very well in America, and like to give back to the community that had given me a shelter," Lutvi said shyly.

"Every day I would pick up leftover pastries, muffins and breads and feed all those wonderful Americans, forced to the streets by the irresponsible ways of their politicians."

A stocky, muscular Mongol approached.

"Doug, please meet my bodyguard Babul, jiu jitsu master and former cop. Anytime you feel in danger, holler if you see him, and I am sure he will be delighted to help."

"Oh, here comes Mr. Staplegun," Lutvi smiled as a middle aged man pushing a cart stopped by.

"Who are you, stranger? You got a name? I am Jason Nazim, also called Mr. Staplegun. You ain't no SSA, ain't you? You better not be one of them motherfuckers, stranger," he growled in anger.

Mr. Staplegun had even richer and more bewildering personal story than Lutvi Bezirganov.

Jason Nazim, a Persian Jew whose family emigrated from Iran after the fall of the Shah, had a two-year stint with the Marines at age of 18 and later re-enlisted, earning high decorations during the first Iraq war.

Born and raised in a strict Muslim country by an Orthodox Jewish family, young Jason was amazed by the intensity of the gentile's world.

"Americans spend six days a week trying to emulate bunch of billionaires, then would go to church on Sunday and pray to a bare foot Rabbi called Immanuel to forgive all their trespasses," he would joke some times.

"I think this is quite incredible, isn't it?"

But when in Rome, you do what the Romans do, so hardworking and practical Jason soon built a successful income tax service in Brooklyn that netted him a few million dollars bank account and comfortable living in the suburbs. Still, so many years after his arrival in New York, the Christian world was taunting him with cultural enigmas he had trouble understanding.

A new dimension of his life was to

become evident as September 11, 2001 catastrophic societal changes impacted his life in ways he never thought possible.

An overzealous bureaucrat in the Homeland Security Department had landed his name on a watch list of possible terror suspects due to what he thought was a name that sounded too Arabic, never mind that he had an Iranian passport and his religious classification was "Jewish." Despite a complaint by his congressman and Rabbi, Jason's fate was already carved in stone as a possible enemy of USA, a proposition so absurd that his friends from the synagogue were left speechless.

Jason was infuriated by the stupidity of those hillbillies who by a strange directive of history had all of a sudden found themselves in position to judge people and cultures they have never heard about.

Then another blow was sent by the Providence.

At age of 42, Jason, who had dizziness spells since his deployment in Iraq due to being stationed near the burning chemical bunkers of Saddam, suffered a fall that left him with numb legs, unable to work and therefore forced to apply for Social Security benefits.

After three years of extensive treatment and therapy, he was back in business but not out of trouble.

The Social Security Administration had paid him $20,376.50 in benefits, and later decided that most of the money must be repaid back due to his income bracket, which he happily agreed to.

Then another government bureaucrat struck out. Apparently not aware that moving a decimal point two places to the right can make a serious difference in one's life, he sent Jason a bill for $2,037,650.00, due immediately.

All appeals turned out to be futile.

"You should pay this amount right away. We know you Arabs are stuffed with money," the case examiner concluded.

An Iraq vet friend of Jason, an employee at the Social Security Administration, had managed to get a peek on his file, just to discover that seventeen people with the same social security number have been illegally receiving benefits for some time, hence explaining the two million dollar slap in the mouth and not a numerical idiocy as suspected previously.

A complaint by his representative, a Democrat and a Jew himself, went to deaf ears.

New York was a sanctuary city, and anyone raising issue with the millions of illegals that had burdened the state with benefits, school tuition and other freebees were labeled "racists" and "bigots", as he had stumbled into a cement block called the American Government and the treachery of the elected politicians.

That was enough for Jason. He had a well arranged fake divorce with his wife, leaving her the real estate and $850,000.00 in investments, depositing $50,000.00 with his attorney to continue the appeals, taking $1,500,000.00 in cash and then vanished in the streets of New York City, money deposited in some fifty safety deposit boxes all around the country.

He had met another veteran named Billy Boston, a man with white hair who looked just like him, a brave American man who passed away last winter during a major snowstorm. Jason called the authorities to pick up his body, but kept Billy's ID in case he may be cornered by the bloodhounds of SSA who by now had issued Court Orders to confiscate his property, property of a decorated Veteran of the first Iraq War, now an outlaw and on the run.

To confuse the Federal agents, he had sent a hand written letter to a vet buddy of his down in Georgia, who in turn sent it back to Jason's attorney, stating that he is depressed and suicidal, on his way down to the Caribbean Islands in search of freedom, a move that hopefully would turn the hound dogs of the SSA away, at least for the time being.

Jason in fact was sharing a comfortable apartment owned by another veteran down on 79th street, everything paid in cash, seeing his wife and family at least twice a week, after precautions were taken to make sure that they were not followed by someone with a crew cut and dark glasses. Still, hanging out around Central Park was a dangerous proposition, so Jason had armed himself with a 1/2-inch Home

Depot staple gun and dog spray as protection in case of trouble.

It did not take long for him to stumble into Princess Lucy Brave and her Imperial Palace, a meeting which exploded into a vicious confrontation between a crazy woman making lightning fast slashing moves destined for his unshaved face and an experienced American Veteran sending a cloud of staples against the enemy, calling her a misfit and an SSA bitch.

Only the peaceful and kind intervention of Lutvi with a box of éclairs in hand saved the day, and ever since, both would sit on an opposite park benches in a sign of silent detente.

"You see, Doug, most of us around here are hiding from the government in one way or another," Lutvi joyfully explained.

"Even Princess Lucy lost everything, including her house upstate when the treachery of the politicians caused the 2008 real estate crash. Here comes another couple of freedom fighters, Pipe Man Joe Sanchez, his dog Sylvester and Sgt. Darnel Williams, also known as the medicine man. Hello Chiefs, say 'Hi' to our new man Doug."

Filthy, unshaven man with missing front teeth smile stopped by, pushing a cart with large pipe protruding prominently behind bags of empty pop cans, small white pooch following on the right, right in front of Williams medicine cart.

"You have some extra chow guys, we ain't eating since morning, and may we be graced with your mercy, Princess Lucy?"

"I have four and a half muffins for you guys, eat some and give the rest to my dear Sylvester," Lucy said, handing the plate Lutvi had just given her.

"Thank you kindly, Princess, thank you very much for saving our day."

"We have been badgered by a bunch of bad asses lately, young punks, you know, tattooed all over, smoking pot, threatening to beat us old folks and drive us out of the park," Pipe Man said.

"Maybe your young man Babul can have word with them, don't you think, Lutvi?"

Doug was starting to like this very much, a real world social unit with its own rules, demands and culture.

"I have to dress Mother Hattie as a homeless person and introduce her to the guys. She will absolutely love them, especially Princess Lucy," he thought, suspiciously looking around, fearing that someone may read his thoughts.

"Here come the punks, a whole bunch of them, sound general quarters, mates, general quarters," Pipe Man cried warily, pulling the steel pipe from his cart.

A group of four young men and two women with shopping carts, filthy and ragged, approached from behind the trees,

Lutvi and friends waited, full with tension, weapons in hand, ready for a fight.

A tall, skinny man with a purple tank top

shirt, tattoos all over and a yellow ring protruding from his nose, laid down the orders.

"You old farts have five minutes to get your asses out, including the blond bitch with a busted smile back there, or we will beat the living daylights out of you right now. This is our park, get out, and get moving, I said right now."

Doug couldn't believe the tension in the air, tension so thick, you could cut it with a knife, yet no one was moving.

Then something extraordinary happened that took everyone by surprise.

Like a tigress defending her cubs, Lucy approached silently, head down as if an attack was imminent, then flew in the air and delivered a kick to the chest of the tall punk so devastating and brute that he fell back and took his flock down, shopping carts and all to the ground.

Lucy grabbed the steel pipe and put it to his neck, a foot on other side.

"You dirty, pee-drenched bastard, you come here one more time, I will cut dog's balls and have them stitched up to your smelly ass, do you hear me, dopes?"

"Get out of here, or Babul will break your knuckles finger by finger."

The punks ran for their dear lives, leaving the carts and trash behind.

"Gentlemen, please fall down on you knees and bow your heads in honor of the Princess of Central Park," Lutvi announced respectfully.

"Now you know why I adore and respect this wonderful lady so much."

"It has been a long and trying day, and this calls for a celebration. I will be back soon with some hot pierogies and iced tea so we can rejoice our victory over the punks," Lutvi promised, and then walked among the trees toward the street.

Operation "Silver Spoon"

A fine art gallery owner by day and a drug dealer by night, Jose Pena-Solis had all his life treasured a story with an elegant and promising beginning, and an ending that was incomprehensibly tragic, creating enigmatic and troubling inferences that had bothered him to this very day.

His grandfather Morris, a vaudeville artist and master pickpocket on the streets of Paris, had snatched a priceless gold pocket watch, Guilloche 1910, just before returning back to England to board the famed ship Titanic on her maiden voyage to New York. Leaving on his rendezvous with destiny, he had the words "To Morris from Edna" engraved on inner back cover, then rubbed the inscription with a pencil on the top page of a letter to be sent to his wife back in the States, creating a sentimental treasure that Jose Pena-Solis had kept to this very day.

Tragically, Morris and hundreds of other souls perished in North Atlantic's most tragic and infamous accident, then forty years after the greatest maritime tragedy in history, the watch miraculously re-appeared in New York, owned by a well-known politician, Councilman Abraham Kreutzer.

Jose Pena-Solis visited one of councilman's town hall meetings, and after flattering his political accomplishments, was allowed to examine the watch he was wearing, just to open the back cover and compare the haunting message with his exact copy, an event that made his heart miss a few beats.

Rage and feelings of betrayal started boiling in his heart.

"Brats of a whore, low life prairie coyotes," he swore in fury.

"Some son of a bitch snatched this priceless possession off my dying grandfather, then sold it on the streets for miserable few dollars, just to pay the rent for a month or two. I must have it back, just to honor the memories of a wonderful man who perished in a terrible tragedy."

A trusted associate of his, Johnny "Hot Rice" Woo, a man whose small China Town gang had specialized in distributing drugs using private safety boxes, highly recommended a set of Manila born and raised twins as the perfect team for the job.

Subic boys Johnny and Lonny Henderson, sons of chief ordinance officer at Subic Bay Naval Station and a Philippine opera star mother, grew in privilege and comfort, educated in the best schools money can buy, making the piano playing their first major passion. By the age of twelve, they had already made a name for themselves in many of the most respected cultural domains, yet a new and troublesome pastime had started to skew their life in a direction one could hardly expect in such cultured and distinguished young men.

The lightning fast fingers of the Subic boys had the strength of an elephant, deadly hit of the cobra and gentle sway of the gay Manila Bay breeze, a gift soon placing them in an environment of snatching and removing things of value from other people, a passion that had soon cascaded into an addiction.

At the age of 18, the CIA had already got wind of their exploits, leading to a cold war caper whereby a prized US microfilm was stolen by a KGB agent just to be snatched back by the Subic boys and then double locked in a US Government safe. After their father's retirement, the boys had found themselves living in New York City, a situation reminiscent to a hungry fox released in a coop full of tasty and overfed chickens where people were laden with luxury items just begging to be taken away for permanent safekeeping.

Even though the Subic boys still did some work for the CIA from time to time, they had created an elaborate system of safe houses full with treasures that would have made the professionals from Ali Baba and the forty thieves green with envy.

So Jose Pena-Solis, deeply honored to be able to work with two living legends of the underworld, offered the Subic boys an incredible sum of $5000.00 for the watch in mint condition, no questions asked.

Doug was told that the two Philippine pick-pockets were actually working together with the rest of the gang in executing important heists, such as the acquisition of a priceless necklace of an opera star and other spectacular hits, events that had raised the suspicion of Sergeant David Kemeny, Chief of Police Criminal Detail at Central Park.

"I know you Subic boys are into all bunch of crooked shit, and one of these days, I will catch you with the goods, then make sure you get so much time upstate so next time you see an ass, it will be yours, in a mirror."

The twins had borrowed a tactic of the prairie dogs of the Kalahari desert, whereby Lonny would run full speed in one direction, and a homeless man named "Windy" run at right angle away from him, thus diverting the attention of everybody, leaving Johnny to snatch the prize from the victim and immediately pass it to Lucy, who would innocently be passing by.

All this risk was of course not for free, and depending on the value of the loot, co-conspirators may be treated to a steak dinner and get a $25.00 cash bonus.

After two months of meticulous stalking of the councilman, it was determined that on the fourth Sunday of every month, he held a town hall meeting followed by a dinner with his most ardent supporters at Delmonico's Steak House. Then he would walk back toward his apartment, always on shady part of the street, many times accompanied by friends and admirers.

The Subic boys had a bad news for Mr.

Pena-Solis.

Actionable historical value of the watch was estimated to be at least $250,000.00; hence the $5000.00 offer was grossly inadequate due to constant surveillance by Sergeant Kemeny and some other unpredictable risks. The recovery fee was raised to $25,000.00 with $5000.00 in services Pena-Solis was to render distributing some inventory down in Miami and Central America, the rest in cash.

"Take it or leave it or no watch at all," was the Subic boy's final offer.

The big, proud heart of Jose Pena-Solis was broken, his big Spanish eyes full with tears.

After weeks of thought and painful deliberations, he finally caved in and gave a green light to the project.

A pivotal part of the heist was to be played by no one but Dr. Woramcke in close cooperation with Lonny and Windy, perpetrators of a distraction that would allow Johnny to approach and grab the watch in a carefully designed commotion.

On "S" day lookout conspirators watched Mr. Kreutzer slowly move trough the crowd on his way back home, followed by a group of admirers, including Lonnie and Windy.

Just feet from the Metropolitan Museum of Natural History, Woramcke entered the stage, approached the Councilman and respectfully requested an autograph, which he was happy to oblige. Then all hell broke lose.

Producing the stupidest smile in the world, Woramcke released the loudest fart of his career, stating, "Hell, I don't even like you, Councilman. I am a Libertarian and cannot stand the Democrats."

Offended beyond belief and well known for his short temper, Mr. Kreutzer lunged at him and missed as Lonnie and Windy, pretending to be outraged by the assault on their favorite politician, jumped at Woramcke and started hitting him.

This was the moment of truth. In the ensuing commotion, Johnny clipped with one lightning move the watch from the chain, immediately passing it to Lucy, who of course was walking in the opposite direction.

As planned well in advance, Lonnie and Windy got into their Kalahari routine, one running parallel, the other at right angle to Central Park West.

But as it had happened with endless precision military operations, there was a nasty surprise.

Unknown to the conspirators, four plainclothes policemen had been tailing the councilman, and soon, all except Lucy were cuffed to the ground right next to her palace.

Doug, an innocent observer of this crime in progress, found himself being frisked by a young cop, who in no time found his NYPD badge.

"Well, what do we have here, partner?"

There was crackling answer in his earpiece, and then he gave Doug a strange look, slowly moving away in the crowd.

Sergeant Kemeny was furious beyond belief.

"They tricked me. Somehow, they snatched the watch of a major NY politician right under my nose."

"You Subic boys just got yourselves a twenty four hour a day nanny. I will tuck you in bed at night and make your cereal in the morning, and when I catch you with the goods, you'll get your asses stuffed in the slammer for so long that you will celebrate the 400th anniversary of City of New York upstate."

But without any evidence, all participants were let go and Lucy hailed as a hero of the day.

Being in bad mood, she requested that the pickpockets provide her with a "charming" dinner date, which the Subic boys proposed to be "Windy," detained briefly by the police and also due a steak dinner at Delmonico's.

This insensitive and offending offer was met with a rage.

"I want Brown Eyes with me or the watch goes right back to Sergeant Kemeny!" she shouted at them.

"You expect the Princess of Central Park to have a dinner with a stinker missing three front teeth whose last shower was at Christmas? I am so mad at you that I will take the damn watch and smash it right now, are you listening to me, Subic punks?"

The twins, feeling the coveted prize slipping from their long, sticky fingers, fell on their knees, begging her to reconsider and talked "Brown Eyes" into being Lucy's date.

Hot potato was now in Doug's lap.

"Lucy, will I be slashed before or after dinner depending on whether the steak was well done or not?" he asked respectfully.

Surprisingly, she mellowed down, taking a long, sensual look at him.

"I am not that bad, you know? Just wanted to spend an evening with someone I like, and that has been a long, long time for me. Would you try to forgive me, Brown Eyes, for being bad to you a few times?"

"I could try, provided that there won't be envelope openers on the dinner table, do you promise, Princess?

Once peace was agreed to, Lucy started walking down to Lutvy's pastry shop to freshen up for the date, and Doug slipped in the Meecham Building to clean up and report the latest news to Mother Hattie.

Suspicion and fear filled her eyes.

"You are having a candlelight dinner at Delmonico's with the same ragged person that put a blade on your throat just two months ago?

"I am sorry Doug, but that is sheer madness, and Robert must be told of this. Maybe he could put someone nearby to make sure there is help, just in case."

For the first time in months, he had to agree, having a gut feeling that his experiment was rapidly approaching the edges of his flight envelope, as pilots like to say.

Despite all grave suspicions, everything turned to be normal from the beginning of the evening as Lucy started opening up with the help of couple glasses of fine wine.

Born in Peking, China, the only daughter of a CIA agent father and an US Air force medical doctor mother, she started practicing wushu martial arts as a child, getting her black belt at the age of twenty three.

At twenty six, Lucy married an Air Force pilot, Ritchie Langille, the nicest guy in the world who gave her all the love she ever dreamed of, in a marriage punctuated by occasional deployments she really did not mind much, just counting the days when he would come back home each time.

Then came the 2nd Iraq War and the biggest blow of her young life. As Ritchie's squadron was approaching the air defenses of city of Mosul, in a one in a million chance, an Iraqi RPG projectile exploded nearby his helicopter, scattering metal fragments that set it on a deadly spin, killing all aboard as his comrades watched in helpless horror.

When two Air force officers came to her front door with the grave news, she could not comprehend the magnitude of the loss, feeling complete numbness and emptiness, incapable of accepting the thought that the man she loved

more than anything in the world was no more.
Then something snapped inside her. With the TV
and all the lights on in the house, she opened the
front door and started walking away, on a cold
and gloomy day in a freezing drizzle, away
toward Central Park.

Somewhere along the way, she stopped
for a cup of coffee in a small roadside restaurant,
just to find herself a victim of a robbery in
progress as two Spanish-speaking vagrants, one
armed with a small revolver and the other with a
knife, grabbed her as a hostage, demanding all
money in the cash register.

The punks should have been much safer if
the police had arrested them since picking a bone
with a Chinese-trained sixth degree wushu master
on the worst day of her life was to give them a
lesson in English they would never forget. The
bandit with revolver in his hand found himself
flying head first through a storefront window. It
shattered to a cloud of razor sharp needles as the
other got a kick in the back of the head that
knocked him unconscious almost immediately.

The next morning Lucy was in front of a
pastry shop, soaked to the bone in a freezing rain,
just a few hundred feet from the tree in Central
Park where Ritchie had proposed to her just four
years ago.

When Lutvy looked through his window
and saw Lucy, his endless and compassionate
soul of a magic prince from the Scheherazade
tales sensed the pain she was going through and

he invited her in to dry off. She was treated with hot coffee and pastries, and then driven to Macy's to get some cold weather clothes.

Her father and CIA detail were on location by 1 PM, but Lucy wouldn't budge.

The daughter of a recently retired assistant director of the CIA could not be allowed to perish on the streets of New York, so Lutvy got a proposal. He would be paid $45,000 a year to provide her with food and shelter, especially in inclement weather, and report any threats against her, day or night.

Being the fine horse thief that he was, Lutvy came up with an even better offer. He would take care of the girl and report to the CIA all current news regarding the Russian Mafia, his UN mission customers and other underground outfits with whom he came in contact with. In exchange, the Feds would offer clemency in case the FBI got wind of his less than religious occupation and activities.

The CIA accepted the offer and also stationed an experienced enforcer, Mongol police captain Babul Unkur, masquerading as Lutvy's bodyguard and personal driver, just in case anything went out of whack.

All seem perfect and safe for all, but it was just an illusion, unable to cure the pain and sense of depression still overwhelming her lonely heart.

Lucy took a deep sip of wine, then put her hands over her eyes and started weeping softly.

Doug could not stand the pain anymore.
He sat next to her, his hands in a warm embrace,
lips kissing her forehead and eyes, whispering,
"Don't cry dear girl, things are to get better, I
promise, very soon."

Then he heard a very, very familiar voice,
a voice like coming from a different dimension.

"I am sorry to disturb you young folks,
just wanted to say a good evening and ask if there
is something the mayor of the great city of New
York could do to make sure that your treasures
are many and follies be few?"

"Good evening, Sir, I am Lucy Brave,
Princess of Central Park, very honored to meet
you," she whispered respectfully.

"Then this would be Prince of Central
Park, wouldn't he?" Mayor Weisberg inquired
carefully.

"I am Douglas Strange, Sir, it is a
privilege."

"You know Doug, I really hate to intrude,
but you look so familiar to me that I am starting
to wonder if I ever knew your father or
grandfather, did I? Perhaps not. At any rate,
please accept my compliments, and I hope you
have a wonderful evening," Mayor Weisberg said
before leaving.

Lucy was bewildered by the encounter.

"Have you ever met this man before,
Doug? I had the feeling that he knows your
family."

"We are very common types, dear." Doug

said jokingly.

"He's probably mixing me up with someone else."

When the dinner was over and they walked slowly back to the park, Lucy stopped, then looked straight in his brown eyes and asked, "Would you mind kissing your date, Doug?"

"I have to admit I am very tempted, but then hate to see my smile scattered over 'don't cross the street on red' sign," he whispered back.

"No karate kicks, pokes in the eyes, knees below the waist, you promise?"

"Stop and close your eyes," she ordered.

Then came a kiss, soft and gentle, sending waves of sensual fire all over his body.

Still in mild shock, he heard her steps fade away among the tress.

Eyes wide open, heart beating fast and mind still trying to comprehend the happenings of this memorable evening, Doug stood in numbness for a while, and then slowly walked back to the Meecham Building.

Mother Hattie was in tears when she heard the story, exclaiming, "I need to meet this sweet child soon, promise me dear, and give her a hug or two. You will introduce me, would you, Doug? I do hope you don't mind."

"Of course, Mother Hattie, at the earliest time I would, that's a promise."

The Assassin

Doug was back in his favorite place next to the tree's adorned palace of Lucy, dressed in torn clothes and with a freshly unshaved face, not far from the edge of the park, hearing hundreds of conversations and observing people passing by, the living soul of life on New York's streets. It turned out to be an uneventful and lonely day with the usual suspects, including Lucy, out of sight, one of those days without a name or story that would be softly swept away by the winds of time, swept away like a faded picture in the endless maze of our mind.

Just around noon, depressed by his loneliness and seeking shelter from the heat, Doug thought of moving his camp behind the trees, away from prying eyes and pulsating street noise, ready for a nap. Hardly a few minutes had passed when he heard noise of someone jogging, and oddly enough, the footsteps stopped, something fell in the brush close to him, then the steps slowly faded away in the distance. The scientific curiosity of Doug started flaming as he carefully crawled out of his hideout to take a look, just to see a plastic bag and a carcass of a dead mouse inside.

"Dirty polluter bastard, son of swine" he thought in disgust, and then noticed that the tummy of the mouse had been carefully sewn out, like in a surgery, immediately raising his suspicion.

43

"My God, this has to be a dead drop," a swirl of emotions swept his thoughts as he retreated back in the brushy hideout.

"Let's wait and see who might show up to pick up the goods."

About a quarter of an hour had passed when he saw a middle aged man with a small metal detector scouring the area for treasure, then coming straight towards him, and the bag was gone.

Face down to the ground, breathing stealthily, Doug waited for the steps to fade away, then carefully peeked from behind the trees to see the man walking rapidly toward the street exit. Suspiciously scanning the surrounding area, just to make sure there was no one tailing him, he started moving quickly from behind one tree to another, keeping the subject in sight and following his hasty retreat. Just at park's edge, Doug felt he was being observed and looked to his left. He though he saw Lucy's face behind the trees, but by then, the man was at the West 72nd street entrance of the subway, ready to disappear in New York's underground, so he had to follow and the chase was on, fast and chillingly cold.

The subject changed routes and subway cars many times, and then joined a group of onlookers admiring a presentation of a subway dance group, while stealthily scouring the crowd for a familiar face. The chase was on again, as he took the route to Brooklyn where he exited the subway in a hurry and hitched a raid in a taxi, forcing Doug to get one also.

"This is turning out to be like a page of a spy novel," he thought, then ordered the driver to follow the car. The breathtaking chase continued for almost an hour as the suspect changed taxis twice, circling around for a while, coming to a stop in front of an old, worn out building. Doug gave the cab driver a hundred and ordered him to park nearby and wait. Across the street, the subject got a cup of coffee from a vending stand, then kept walking around, sat down for a while on a sidewalk bench reading a newspaper, smoked a cigarette and got another cup of coffee.

"He must be waiting for a contact," Doug thought, and then went back to the cab, giving the driver another hundred. Finally, there was development across the street as a taxi dropped a young woman and the couple entered trough the side door of the building. Doug was able to snap a picture with his camera and then went back to the taxi on the way to his base of Central Park. In the rush of the chase, he had not observed that a man on the third floor of the building, armed with what appeared to be large binoculars, was observing all street activities, including his taxi, an omission that was to prove fateful in just a few hours later.

Lt. La Paglia was skeptical when he heard the caper.

"Most likely a bunch of drug dealers making a contact, but I will notify the Intelligence section and request they take a look at this report."

So everything was back to normal as Doug had managed to slip in Meecham's building to download his latest data observations, then go back to his hollow next to Lucy's palace, taking a short nap with her just few feet on his right. No more than ten minutes later he felt being pulled roughly to his side and heard Lucy screaming, "Watch out!" as a swirling ax passed just an inch from his left temple, lodging itself deeply in the tree's trunk. Still drowsy and unable to comprehend the brutality of the attack, he saw Lucy walking in the air toward a dark clad assassin, twisting her climb to avoid blow from another ax swirling on the way, but it was too late. A shower of blood sprinkles fell over his face as he tried to slow her fall. Then out of nowhere, Babul Unkur was on location, sweeping the assassin off his feet and kicking out a large knife, but the man was a professional and back up in a flash, pointing a gun with a silencer at him. A spree of gunshots popped out, and the assassin went down, leaving a curtain of terror and silence behind. Sgt. Williams came running with his medic bag, skillfully cutting Lucy's right arm sleeve to expose a slash from the elbow to the shoulder with blood rushing out.

"Press this gauze against her arm and don't let go or she may go into a shock from the blood loss," he ordered.

"I will try to turn her slightly to her left to see if there is injury to the rib cage."

The terror of the attack stopped the flow of time in Doug's mind, and he just clung to Lucy's arm, desperately trying to reduce the severe blood loss, as sirens of emergency vehicles and sound of a chopper seemed to converge to the park. When Mayor Weisberg and Commissioner Murphy finally arrived, Lucy was already on a gurney, oxygen mask snapped on her face as two medics were feverishly working to stabilize her for an airlift to the hospital. Blood covered Doug, still in shock and holding her arm, afraid that if he let her go, she may never come back to him, unable to comprehend the senselessness of the attack. Two mini hatchets, covered with blood and imbedded deeply into the tree's trunk, lit a fire of fury in the eyes of Mayor Weisberg, who was wearing his service weapon in a side holster, for the first time in Doug's memory.

"I went to war and spent decades to make my city safe from violence, just to see some worthless SOB butcher this fine young woman's arm and threaten the life of my beloved godson. I want to know who is he working for, Commissioner, then I will make it my personal business to give them a lesson in good old fashion American brutality and justice," he said in rage.

"And you, young man, take care of your girl, and we will be talking about this later," were the last words Doug heard before the Medevac chopper ascended in the starry heavens above

New York on the way to the hospital helipad. Running after the emergency crew rushing Lucy into the ICU through endless doors and brightly lit hallways amplified the terror and despair that had started in the park, ending abruptly when an attendant handed out a clean up kit and asked him to take a chair.

Then a strange and eerie peace set in because this was a private wing of the hospital and Doug was alone, all alone in front of a nursing station in a stony silence interrupted by sudden wind of distant conversations, beeping sounds of life monitors and muted pagers relaying critical orders. Drawn down and crushed by the stress of the evening, he had fallen asleep for a while in a domain of dreams of red lights and screams for help. Then he felt someone touching his arm gently.

"Lucy, is that you?" he asked, trying to open his heavy eyelids into the bright lights of the waiting room.

It was an attendant, handing out a change of clothes pack and a dinner courtesy of Mayor Weisberg.

"Can you please tell me if Lucy Brave is alright?" Doug whispered, a desperate question sounding almost like a prayer.

"We are still working on her," she smiled.

"We will let you know. Just try to clean up, have your dinner and everything will be fine."

Refreshed and full with new hope, Doug took notice of the time. It was 3:15 AM, so he decided to wait for the nursing shift change before making further inquiries.

When he woke up at around six, there was a new crew of nurses and attendants at the station who were not particularly helpful or kind at all.

"Are you a family of this patient, and can you identify yourself as such?" a male nurse barked at him.

" We are not allowed by the HIPAA law to disclose patient information without written consent. I must ask you to leave or you will be escorted out by our security officers."

Police badge of a Captain in NYPD was a definite attention getter.

"She was airlifted to another location," the nurse smiled.

"You need to file a written request through your department for further information."

A taxi cab dropped Doug in front of Lutvy's pastry shop around seven in a drizzle coming down from low, gray clouds just above the trees, as he could clearly see Woramcke and the others tucked under a tent the police had left behind. If he ever needed someone to talk to, this had to be the day, so he rented a whole party cart loaded with four pots of assorted coffee, stacks of pancakes and other goodies, then pushed it across the street.

The guys were amazed by his fortune.

"Did you win a lottery or something, stranger? This is a quite a heap of love you got yourself into."

"My aunt gave me two hundred dollars last night," Doug laughed.

"I hope you don't mind sharing it with me."

So they sat under the tent in an endless and sadly monotonous rain drizzle, sipping hot coffee and sharing the sweets, reminiscing the good old days when Lucy was around, around a group of people the Providence had brought together to face the peaks and valleys of their destiny, under the majestic trees of Central Park.

Then there was a journey of loneliness again, since his cover had been blown and he could no longer stay in the park with the usual crowd. The last week of October was a row of tense twelve-hour days, every hour spent in preparation of his dissertation, scheduled for November 4, 2010. The defense actually turned surprisingly well, considering that the vaunted Chair of the Examination committee Dr. Gould asked only one relatively hostile question, thus giving Doug clear sailing to the end when a wave of applause filled up Knox Hall, an expression of crowd's enthusiastic support for their favorite teacher and friend. Dr. Stafford had some twenty books to give away, and when the last student came to get a copy, he did not recognize her and asked for her name.

"Natalie Mac Ain," she said gently, her beautiful eyes glowing behind rose colored glasses, brown hair tucked under a white woven French barrette adorned with two red rubies.

Doug watched her turn around and walks away, then a wave of emotion swept his heart after the incredibly beautiful overtones of her voice flashed a memory of someone he had been thinking of since the days in the park.

"How is your shoulder?" he asked softly.

"Actually, it's getting better by the day," she answered and then froze in surprise.

There was only one thing to do. He offered Natalie his wide open embrace, and she fell sobbing into it, just to see Mother Hattie and Mayor Weisberg on other side with eyes bigger than a new moon.

"Do I sense a duet, children?" Mayor Weisberg inquired cautiously.

"Oh dear child," Mother Hattie whispered, almost in tears.

"I wanted to give you a hug for such a long, long time. Doug, please get out of my way, would you?"

"Be careful with her, Mother, she is still in recovery, don't you forget."

With Mother Hattie and Major Weisberg gone, Doug and Natalie walked back to Delmonico's, sharing a bottle of wine over lunch as his eyes adored her in the curious dance of the candlelight, creating a sense of silent music of incredible beauty and love that he had never felt before.

"I hate to bring in an unpleasant memory that may cause you pain, but who was the hatchet-throwing assassin working for? I nearly lost my mind when I saw you go down that evening."

Natalie searched his face with her eyes, like being afraid that her answer may hurt him.

"The CIA was tracking for some time a gang of North Korean tough guys involved in smuggling triggers for nuclear weapons. The dead drop you witnessed and reported to Lt. La Paglia was ignored, leaving you right in the cross hairs of an assassination attempt. You of course had no idea what was going on until I saw a man just twenty feet away from you and intervened, just to get hurt in the scuffle."

"And the watch of Councilman Kreutzer?" Doug inquired cautiously.

"Jose Pena-Solis is a small fish, but his brother in law Delgado was a front for a major foreign intelligence service on the lookout for acquisition of major US secrets. The CIA wanted to convince Pena-Solis that the Subic boys are such fine crooks that Delgado could hire them to snatch the data manual of the multi-node parallel H hyper-processor used in our nuclear subs, a tasty treat that they were foolish enough to fall for. As for the poor councilman, the Subic boys will miraculously slip the priceless watch back in his pocket just a day before Hanukah, I assure you."

"I need to give another loving hug, my dear," Doug offered his warm embrace again.

"You saved my life and could have lost yours on the way, dear child," he thanked her with a kiss, kissing her beautiful eyes.

"My life without you would have been meaningless, and I was willing to sacrifice it if needed be, just to be with you," she whispered, eyes full with tears.

There was another long and sensual embrace, followed by silence as they watched the dance of candlelight's play a magic story on the walls around them. Then he asked something that had been on his mind for a long, long time. Doug was carrying the engagement ring of his mother, an intricate ring of white gold, encrusted in diamonds and red rubies.

"Natalie Mac Ain, do you feel strong enough to be asked a question of life and love?"

"Yes," she replied gently.

"Natalie, would you please marry me? I have my dear mom's engagement ring, ready for your finger."

She held the ring in her trembling hands, looking for a long time at the dance of lights as they were bouncing the colors of the rainbow the diamonds and the rubies were radiating, tears streaming down her face.

"Yes, Doug, I fell for you the moment I saw you in the park. Yes, I want to spend my life with you."

They held hands together in a circle of love, afraid that if they let go, then they would never be able to see each other again.

The Big Day

The wedding of Doug and Natalie was set for the 15th of January 2011; exactly forty-three years to the day Doug's parents had exchanged their vows in a small chapel in Napa Valley, just before the deployment to Vietnam. A flurry of tense preparations followed advice from loved ones determined to make this wedding day not only a day to remember, but also a nocturnal attempt to honor those fallen or departed, the loving memories of whom were deeply ingrained in their minds.

After the hatchet incident, Doug's cover was blown and there was no need to hide anymore, so he arranged for some of the guys to get food and shelter provided by the Meecham Foundation. Stormy and Sanchez got new dentures for their busted front teeth and Woramcke was appointed adviser to Meecham Trust for the Arts, the whole gang now ready for the happy days ahead.

The list of VIP guests was overwhelming, including Major Stafford's wing man in Vietnam, Captain Robert Weisberg, DFC with oak leaf cluster, Lt. General John Hastings, US Air Force, Major Graham Carter, now Chief of Satellite Intelligence at the CIA and finally Captain Erik Swenson, a President of a major aerospace company, the last surviving four members of their squadron during the Haiphong

Harbor bombing campaign. The commissioner of the Social Security Administration Miles Sartini, his lovely wife Ines and mother Mabel were also present, and so was the Federal Judge for State of New York and Doug's second cousin, Annabel Hoskins.

A host of other guests, including the Subic boys under the watchful eye of Mother Goose Sgt. Kemeny, Sgt. Williams, Sgt. Jason Nazim and finally Lutvy Bezirganov, who was hardly holding his tears when Lucy was led to the altar by her white haired father.

The music by New York's finest musicians and performers brought tears to the eyes of many as Mother Hattie and Mabel Sartini were trying to keep their composure until that magic moment the priest would speak the words everyone was waiting for. The pinnacle of the emotional steeple was a performance by vocal group of one of Henry Mancini's greatest hit, "Moon River", the same song that had graced the wedding of Doug's parents forty-three years ago. After the newlyweds exchanged vows and their wedding rings, words from the pulpit announced the creation of the loving union of Doug and Natalie, and the magic moment everyone was longing for.

"Ladies and Gentlemen, it is my high privilege to introduce to you Dr. and Mrs. Stafford, The Prince and Princess of Central Park."

A wave of applause swept the chapel as

kisses, embraces, handshakes and tears drowned the emotional crowd, an end of a relationship born in tragedy turned into love that was tough to comprehend.

When Doug was leading his new bride out for photo ops, he could not help but observe the brilliance in the eyes of the Subic boys and clearly uncomfortable Sgt. Kemeny.

"My God, their mouths must be watering looking at all this jewelry and valuables around here. I hope they keep their word and don't offend Lucy in any way."

A black limousine pulled over to take newlyweds away for the reception in downtown's Hilton Hotel, when suddenly a file of black clad, heavily armed Federal agents penetrated the police line, set-up by order of Commissioner Murphy. Balding, plumb Federal Agent flashed a badge in the face of Lt. La Paglia.

The Lieutenant was not impressed at all.

"An obvious China Town forgery, cue ball. Do you see the signs out there stating this is a police line? Get behind them or I will have your bald headed ass arrested and I mean right now."

Having noticed the commotion, Commissioner Murphy and the Mayor joined Lt. La Paglia.

"Sir Mayor Weisberg, I am special agent Gerald Mooney and very sorry to intervene in your festivities, but we have a Court Order for the arrest of one Jason Nazim, a member of your wedding party."

To say that the Mayor was unpleasantly surprised by this blatant and unwelcome intrusion is simply an understatement, yet on one of the happiest days in his life he found civility to deflect the attack to someone who was clearly the person best qualified to handle it.

"Your Honor, can you please take a look at this question of jurisprudence?" he called on Judge Annabel Hoskins.

"I believe one of Doug's friends is about to be arrested."

Special Agent Mooney was in for some rough treatment.

"I don't recall ever signing a Court Order for the arrest of Mr. Nazim, and it is indicated here that this document is on file with my office. Can you please tell me who signed this Order?" the Judge snapped angrily.

"Your Honor, we had a request for a Court Order on file with your office, and anticipating your approval and signature, we decided that we have enough justification to proceed with the arrest."

"Who is "we," Agent Mooney, and who in the world gave you permission to anticipate my approval? Are you aware that the Social Security Administration settled this case under the direct supervision of Commissioner Miles Sartini a month ago and he personally signed the final draft? I cannot believe that you have the audacity to show up with an armed police detail, offend this party on the happiest day of their lives, ignore procedures and embarrass my office?" Judge Annabel Hoskins was clearly rattled by agent's inconsistency.

Listening to the conversation and enjoying every moment of it, Sgt. Kemeny had a brilliant idea.

"I am about to forget some of your indiscretions, Subic boys, if you would snatch the badge and gun of this asshole Mooney."

The twins looked at him with deep suspicion.

"Are you setting us up, Sergeant?"

"In front of all those VIPs, this would be a suicide."

"No, I mean it guys, you have my word of honor, snatch his badge and gun. I know the Mayor will be delighted, I mean now."

Johnny stepped forward, grabbed agent Mooney by the shoulders, and landed a big kiss on his bald head.

"Hey Roger girl, how you doing, dear? I ain't seen you for a long time, long time, love. Lonny, say "Hi" to Roger, would you bro? Remember that passionate weekend we spent with her in Long Island?"

Sergeant Kemeny couldn't believe what was happening, seeing the boys giving agent Mooney a warm embrace.

"Dear Lord, these two will clean Mooney out of his underwear. I wonder what the Mayor will have to say about this."

Mooney's gun and badge were already in

Lonnie's hands and moving along the gauntlet, on the way to Mayor Weisberg.

It was time to strike.

"Your Honor, perhaps we ought to ask Agent Mooney to identify himself, don't you think?" Mayor Weisberg said acidly.

"May I see your badge, Agent Mooney?" Judge Hoskins pressed angrily.

The poor man was already stupefied by the Subic boys' attack, just to find himself in an even bigger trouble, if that was humanely possible.

"I am very sorry, Your Honor, but I must have left my badge and personal weapon in the office. I will be glad to satisfy your request at a later time, if I may?" the voice of agent Mooney was trembling in fear.

Mayor Weisberg put the badge and gun right in his face.

"These are your badge and personal weapon, aren't they? Our officers recovered it from your two lovers a moment ago."

Johnny and Lonny fell down on their knees, eyes full of tears, begging for mercy.

"Sir Mayor, Your Honor, he slipped the items to us, we swear on the Bible. He did, he just did."

Now was the time for Judge Hoskins to deliver cou'de gra.

"You often share your Federal badge and weapon with your lovers, do you not, Agent Mooney? Let me speak slowly so you don't miss a word."

Mother Hattie and Mabel Sartini interrupted the inquisition, stepping up in front of the crowd.

"Your Honor, would it be a violation of the law if we slapped Agent Mooney with a scarf or perhaps a purse, just to say thanks for his intrusion?"

"I am afraid an assault on a Federal officer is a felony, but gently wiping out the big drops of sweat on his bald head would be construed as giving him comfort under severe duress, something I would wholeheartedly endorse," the Judge admonished.

Mother Hattie and Mabel gently wiped agent Mooney's face and forehead, joined by Sanchez and Stormy who had removed their brand new dentures, offering the poor man a haunting missing front teeth smiles, accompanied by hissing animal sounds, reminiscent of two young baboons coming into heat.

"All right you all, that's enough compassion for one day," the Judge intervened curtly.

" Agent Mooney, I would like to see you on Monday at 10 AM in my office with supervisory agent Lumley. Prepare a written explanation why a team of armed agents under your command, one holding a large metal ram, would show up at a wedding sponsored by His Honor Mayor Weisberg with a deficient Court Order, and why your personal badge and weapon were surrendered to civilians. And in conclusion, if I were you, I would almost certainly consider a name change. Because when I am done with this case, you will be named Mr. Gooney instead of Agent Mooney! Now get your hound dogs out of my face."

Wild applause erupted as agent Mooney and his posse retreated in disarray.

"Auf Wiedersehen, Mooney liebchen, au revoir, goodbye, dosvidania, you chrome dome pencil pushing morons," the gang from Central Park mocked and whistled at them, led by clearly relieved Sgt. Nazim.

Doug was kind of embarrassed by the crowd's rowdiness.

"I am sorry for this unruly goodbye to Agent Mooney, ladies and gentlemen, but those guys have been pushed around by the Feds for years, sleeping in the park rain or shine, and I guess this is a little way to vent that pent-up anger held deep inside of them."

"Please try to understand and forgive them if you would, please."

"Do you forgive them, Natalie dear?"

She had an answer for the crowd.

"As Princess Lucy of Central Park, I hereby forgive and grant clemency to you all my friends. Now let's go to the reception, have a good time and do some good old fashion rock and roll. Doug, dear, lead the way,"

When the happy couple and friends finally arrived at the Hilton Hotel reception room, it became evident that Mayor Weisberg and Mother Hattie had a pleasant surprise for all.

Not only a world famous chef was hired to prepare a constellation of culinary delights already adorning the guest tables, but a twenty piece band joined by twelve member singing group was to offer a musical journey from the 60s to the present, a journey of memories and love many of the guests remembered vividly.

Sgt. Nazim, Sgt. Williams and "Pipe Man" Chief Petty Officer Sanchez were in uniform again, three American warriors, medals shining on their chests.

Subic boys and Lutvy Bezirganov were also present, as the boys swore in all Holy Books, past and present, that nothing, even a silver spoon, would not be found delinquent until the next morning, but not after.

Now that the whole family was together again, and not under a pouring rain, ready to dance the night away in celebration of the wedding of their beloved friends, Douglas Meecham Stafford III and Natalie Mac Ain, formerly known as Lucy Brave, The Prince and Princess of Central Park.

But the persistent and loving care with which Mother Hattie and Mayor Weisberg had worked to make this event an affair to remember, became evident when the orchestra started playing the theme from "Moulin Rouge" as the newlyweds elegantly glided on the dance floor. Suddenly, the lights in the ballroom dimmed softly, changing the background to wavy Turkish blue, and then a whisper like clamor covered the hall as the images of Major Stafford and Isabel appeared on the screen above, sharing their first dance on that memorable day in 1968.

Mother Hattie and Mabel Sartini could not hold back the tears, tears of remembrance and tears of joy that Doug and Natalie finally found love and happiness that had evaded them for so long.

The next day, the newlyweds were at LaGuardia Airport, where a sleek Gulfstream Jet was to take them to their honeymoon in Vietnam.

All his life and despite his enormous wealth, Doug had never admired anything of material value, just spent lifetime searching for that elusive steeple of truth that can lock or unlock a man's heart and bless his search for happiness and contentment.

But as the jet accelerated on the runway and rapidly rose into the endless sky, for the first time in his life he had unchained himself from his past, holding hands with Natalie in a circle of love, eyes full with tears of joy that finally the Providence had blessed them with the fountain of peace he had prayed for an eternity.

18088160R00038

Made in the USA
San Bernardino, CA
28 December 2014